George Douglas Brewerton

**Fitz Poodle at Newport; an incident of the season**

George Douglas Brewerton

**Fitz Poodle at Newport; an incident of the season**

ISBN/EAN: 9783337156534

Printed in Europe, USA, Canada, Australia, Japan

Cover: Foto ©Andreas Hilbeck / pixelio.de

More available books at **www.hansebooks.com**

# FITZ POODLE AT NEWPORT;

## AN INCIDENT OF THE SEASON.

BY

### GEORGE DOUGLAS BREWERTON.

> " If there's a hole in a' your coats,
>   I rede ye tent it ;
> A chiel's amang ye takin' notes,
>   And, faith, he'll prent it."
>
>                                   BURNS.

CAMBRIDGE:

PRINTED AT THE RIVERSIDE PRESS.

1869.

## NOTA BENE.

Entered in accord with Congressional Act
In the District Clerk's Office, so please note the fact,
Of the State of Rhode Island, in language quite terse,
And withal inconvenient to weave into verse.
Of this we feel certain, Eighteen Sixty-nine
Are the figures that noted the year at the time.
So be it remembered 'tis the author's own function
To be ruined by " Fitz " — so beware an injunction.
And to all whom these presents with greeting may come
A caution we give, though you may think it fun:
Don't meddle with this our poetical thunder;
'Tis best " Nitro G." — so beware of a blunder.
And now, lest this entry should not hold in verse,
We'll put it in language more legal and terse;
So below see it printed in lawyer-like prose,
Though we fancy our stanza more gracefully flows.

To

## GEN. CHARLES COLLINS VAN ZANDT,

OF NEWPORT, R. I.

DEAR COLLINS:—I never read a production of yours without a better understanding of what true poetry means. I confess that I envy the power with which your facile pen weaves into glowing fabrics the raw material of the brain. They need but one added charm, and find it in the oratorical grace with which, in the presence of an audience, your eloquence adorns the offspring of an ever genial and sympathetic heart.

As a token of my remembrance of our life-long friendship, I have ventured to dedicate to you this poem. If it find favor in your sight, it will more than compensate the labor of

Your sincere friend,

THE AUTHOR.

STUDIO, NEWPORT, R. I., October 26, 1869.

## GRACE BEFORE MEAT.

"GRACE before meat," if meat should
be found;
If not, the comparison falls to the ground,
And but for the freedom to tread on some toes,
Our Preface perchance might be written in
prose :
A "poetical *license*," — yet when taken out,
Or under what law, is a matter of doubt.
Our *subject* is broad as the billows that fling
Their arms round the green isle whose summer
we sing,
Free as the air that humanity breathes,
High as the heaven, and deep as the seas;
The old story still, as the centuries creep, —
The ulcers of pride that lie festering deep

In the hearts of the careless, the giddy, and vain
Who receive of their fellows, yet give not again,
Whose lives are a vacuum nothing can fill,
Forgetting they're only God's tenants at will,
Stewards whom the Master each moment may
      call
To account for their talents, and render up all.
If with a free pen we appear to have sketched,
Remember our subject is never *far*-fetched,
For the journey is swift from the brain to the
      hand,
And many the fancies that rise at command ;
Nor think that we toil without purpose or plan,
As with critical vision our labor you scan ;
Though, were it allowed to apologize here,
We'd endeavor to tickle your merciful ear
By pleading poor Modesty's ancient excuse,—
Pen and ink out of gear and rusting for use.
Enough that we realize our work is half done,
And only regret it was ever begun.

And now for what we're about to receive,
May each reader prove grateful, nor suddenly
      leave
A repast to which all are freely invited,
For our dishes, true snobs, are unused to be
      slighted ;
And your host, after proving and ardently
      pressing,
Might grieve to have wasted both dinner and
      blessing.

## PRELUDE.

THINK not of summer dreams I sing,
  Or on the high heroic wing
  My Muse may hope to rise and soar
Above the low and level floor
Where Commonplace sees common things;
But though our little tea-bell rings
While others swing the tocsin loud,
That calls each worshipper to crowd
Some shrine where highest art shall raise
New monuments their skill to praise,
We do our work with lance-like pen
To probe the hurts of Upper-ten,
And thus perchance the wound to cure
By letting out the cause impure.
O could my Muse "the giftie gie them
To see themselves as ithers see them!"
But in this world we often find,
He sees the best who stands behind
The mighty looking-glass of Fashion,
That mirror ever stained by passion,
Where envy, hate, and ceaseless strife
Divorce the husband from the wife,
Make home a hell and friends a curse,
Then take the vices in to nurse.

# FITZ POODLE AT NEWPORT.

## AN INCIDENT OF THE SEASON.

UR hero may boast of a lofty line,
    Though his grandsire slipped from a
       scaffold,
Ending his fall by a twist in the spine,
  And a *drop* that e'en surgery baffled.
For the doctors discovered a fracture compound,
'Twixt the second and third of the vertebra found.
To give the story as told at the club,
  By Fitz Poodle, the innocent martyr,
By way of reply to bitter MacSnub,
  Who delights in performing the Tartar.
"He was speaking a piece," though quite in
    the dark,
Having drawn on a night-cap by way of a lark;
But the carpenter fastened the floor in a way
Which soon brought about the event of the day,
For the scaffolding broke, and Poodle *Grand-père*
Was caught by a rope that hung dangling there.
But *where* by that stout cord he managed to
    swing,
Is to touch with rude hand on a delicate thing.

We are told he was talking in accents quite
    loud,
On topics befitting the place and the crowd,
When the *accident* happened that silenced his
    tongue,
For all but Fitz Poodle declare he was *hung*.

At least he was buried, and Poodle James Peter,
The father of Fitz and a regular eater,
Was left a lone orphan and out of employ,
With a stomach and hunger, — bad things for
    a boy.
He was puzzled a little to sup and to dine,
Having nothing to eat and abundance of time;
So when Sirloin, the butcher and pork-packer
    too —
The fellow who sits in the red velvet pew —
Offered Peter a place, and he might have done
    worse,
He preferred a full meal to a ride in the hearse.
Now Peter had ever an eye bright and keen,
A sharp eye for business, as soon will be seen,
For he managed old Sirloin to carve in a way
That quite won the heart of one Mistress O'Flay,
Half-sister to Sirloin, a widow to boot,
Who called her first husband, when living, a
    brute.
But when he was dead, the case was reversed;
She vowed that no babe was more tenderly
    nursed
Than her darling O'Flay, the dearest, the best —

Here up went her kerchief, and sobs drowned
    the rest.
Now this widow was buxom, and Peter was
    young,
With a fine pair of legs and a flattering tongue ;
And O'Flay had left money, a nice little sum,
For he gambled in stocks, and, more singular,
    won.
If the lady was solid, why, so was her pelf ;
So Peter concluded to venture himself ; .
Proposed, was accepted, and married of course,
Yet but for her wealth would have sued for
    divorce ;
When — just as his trials had verged on de-
    spair —
Dame Poodle presented a son and an heir,
And then, in a highly considerate way,
Took her leave of this world on the following
    day.
Old Poodle — we trust he will pardon the slip —
Still talks of her virtues with tremulous lip ;
She had of this cold world so little of leaven,
He had long felt the saint was a subject for
    heaven ;
Had expected to see her go up without wings,
Till he grew quite resigned to the aspect of
    things.
So since his affliction it hardly seems strange
That most people think he has met with a
    change.

Meanwhile young Poodle was cooling his color,
And cutting his teeth without aid from his
    mother;
While his father waxed rich, grew pompous and
    proud,
And forgot the old time when under a cloud.
But still there was something of shop in his
    way;
He had dealt in cold cuts for many a day;
His work had been slashing, through tendon
    and nerve,
Through brain and through sinew, his purpose
    to serve.
What wonder the habit should harden him still
To forget the poor heart-strings he severed
    might thrill?
But enough of old Poodle: he gathers his
    wealth;
Let us hope that erelong he'll be gathered
    himself.

Fitz Poodle was weaned in a summary way,
Though men at the club have offered to lay
A wager the fellow was still out to nurse.
They concede that his weakness is not of the
    purse,
And MacSnub has remarked that though sim-
    ply a fool,
Our hero might learn in Necessity's school;
That a doctor of old had suggested the way,
When he said, " Live on sixpence, and earn it
    each day."

But this is decided, that as to his head,
His brain-pan is soft as a new feather-bed,
And his heart so defiled by the dross of his
        wealth,
That the man cannot even be true to himself.
Be this as it may, with his folly or vice,
And the world has enough of his kind to suffice,
He stands as a type of a class who pretend
To hold themselves higher than those they
        offend.

How Fitz Poodle passed safely through measles
        and rash,
And bragged to the boys of his pony and cash,
What progress he made in acquiring knowledge
Of meanness at school and vices at college,
How he wasted, and gambled, and sometimes did
        worse,
Are things much too common to weave into
        verse.
Suffice it to say that he grew up a man;
We don't like the word, for it injures our plan;
For a puppy is one thing, a man is another,
Though Darwin may fancy the monkey a brother.

And now, as the reader perchance is a lady,
We'll sketch from a photograph, taken by Brady,
Of our hero arrived at the advent of twenty, —
A very ripe age if your greenbacks prove plenty;
For life is a hot-house, where fruit may be
        forced,

Though many the blossom through rottenness
 lost.
Imagine a youth with carroty hair,
A thin pair of legs, and the vacantest stare,
With a nose somewhat large, and withal slightly
 red, —
Perchance its complexion was caught from his
 head, —
With a weak crop of whiskers, quite English in
 style,
Whose care served their purpose, his time to
 beguile;
But though nature proved chary and niggard
 in gift,
His tailor, more gracious, lent Poodles a lift;
For his coats were unrivaled, his vests quite *au
 fait*,
And his breeches a wonder unmatched in their
 day.
'Tis said that the flower with least of perfume,
Is most gorgeous in blossom, most brilliant in
 bloom;
E'en so the Fitz Poodles put on to the back
Each outer adornment, to make up the lack
Of the incense arising from virtue and sense;
In a word, shield their weakness with silly pre-
 tence.


Fitz Poodle's papa had a place by the sea,
A cottage *ornée* — he might have had three;
For his gilt-paper virtues were known to the
 ring.

Each stock that he bulled was a promising
  thing;
But alas for the holders who found him a bear:
When lord of the panic with truculent air,
The widow and fatherless pleaded in vain
To a heart that felt only the maxims of gain.

The season was spring, and the weather quite
  mild,
The heavens looked pure as a babe undefiled,
With slow drifting billows of feathery cloud,
Whose breakers of pearl seemed to jostle and
  crowd,
As through the soft ether they floated away,
With here a bright island and there a blue bay;
Fitz Poodle was passing a night at the club,
With Augustus Redower, a friend from the Hub,
Whose legs led the German, an intricate maze,
Which he who attempts should look well to his
  ways.
Fitz Poodle begins, "Au Gus, do you know,
I think that to Newport this season we'll go;
So drop us a line, and by Jove we will meet
When we get the old gentleman out of the
  street;
For summer's the season, you see, for repose,
And business grows dull, as my governor knows;
So we'll make up a party with Towzer and
  Fearing,
And bring down the blacks with the new patent
  gearing.

Then, if the old man is encouraging loans,
We'll drop into Watson's and rattle the bones."
Redower assented, for dear Mrs. Aram,
With two charming daughters, Carlotta and
        Fan,
Who suited his step in the dance to a hair,
Had taken a cottage, and meant to be there;
So the bargain was made, and the first of July
Was fixed for their meeting ere Gus said good-by.

The roses of June found Fitz Poodle arrayed
In a travelling suit by his Schneider just made,
On the deck of a steamer, the *Bristol*, of course,
With good entertainment for biped and horse.
Next morning behold him arrived at the wharf,
With a carriage in waiting, in haste to be off
To the villa suburban that looks o'er the deep,
Where his night trip enhances the blessings of
        sleep.

The season advances; the church on the hill,
Shut up for the winter, once more gets its fill
Of sinners in satin, who flock to declare
Their creed differs much from the clothing they
        wear;
For while they renounce all pomp and vain-
        glory,
Their milliner's bill tells a far different story.
Still the singing is perfect, the music divine,
Though some deem the Catholic better in time;
But when the dear pastor the pulpit ascends,

His manner so winning, all caviling ends,
And 'tis really delightful, when asked out to dine,
To feel that his blessing has prefaced the wine.
The Atlantic is open, the Ocean House too,
And Cozzens buys stock of the tasteful and new
For Dives, who comes bringing servants and all,
With daughters to flourish at party or ball,
While old Newport puts forth her best foot to
        receive
The guests whom she welcomes for what they
        may leave.

Fitz Poodle had rested and got out his clothes,
And tried the last wash for his ruby-red nose,
When Redower arrived to open the ball ;
So they ordered the horses at Aram's to call.
They found the dear creatures at home when
        they came,
For Fan was Redower's particular flame ;
While as to Fitz Poodle, they both knew full
        well,
He was reckoned a catch, as their father could
        tell ;
For Aram was anxious to get his girls married,
A hope that too often had sadly miscarried,
For Carlotta was thirty, and Fannie had been
Twenty-one to a day since the year she grew
        thin.
The damsels were dressed to suit the occasion,
In toilet so rich, we forbear the relation ;
For both were investments on sale for the season,

With trappings thrown in for an excellent
 reason, —
Accomplishments too ; but 'twould lengthen our
 verse,
If the list of their *extras* we here should re-
 hearse.
Suffice it to say they both simpered and smiled,
While our gay cavaliers a brief hour beguiled
With small talk and flattery, gross and dis-
 tasteful,
For of that which costs nothing we're apt to
 be wasteful.

And now, lest the reader find cause for com-
 plaint,
We'll pencil a sketch, which, though feeble and
 faint,
May serve to present these young ladies more
 fully,
Though Fitz Poodle declares they are " per-
 fectly bully " —
A slangy expression we cannot indorse,
For we've heard the same title prefixed to a
 horse.
Carlotta was dark, and quite Spanish in style,
With a good set of teeth and perpetual smile,
While Fannie, the younger, was shrewish and
 thin,
With nose *retroussé* and a long pointed chin.
'Tis said in affinities opposites meet, —
In which case a row is a positive treat, —

That differing souls love each other the best,
And only the jarring by Hymen are blest.
Be this as it may, Gus and Fan seem united,
While Fitz with Carlotta is greatly delighted.
In short, he was smitten, poor sensitive youth,
No novel event, if we publish the truth,
For our hero was spoony; yet butterfly bred,
He would sip of each flower that grew on the
    bed ;
Yet of woman's devotion, her love, and her trust,
He knew scarcely more than a worm of the
    dust ;
For his soul was a cistern a dew-drop might
    fill,
And his heart in himself had its tenant at will.


'Twas proposed and agreed that the party should
    reach
At ten on the morrow the brown bathing beach,
Where, with marvellous costume, and bluey-white
    lip,
The children of fashion go down for their dip.
Fitz Poodle and Gus would have shortened the
    time,
Discussing the theme as they sat o'er their wine,
But the hours go round in the old-fashioned
    way,
And heed no petition for haste or delay.
Yet the morn came at last, and the equipage too,
The ladies in white and the servants in blue;
And great was the flutter amid the gay throng,

When close to the billows the carriage was borne,
With a glitter of panels and swift-flashing wheels,
While Fitz Poodle full many a tender glance
    steals,
And makes an engagement for croquet and tea
With charming Carlotta, his dark *vis-à-vis.*

The tickets are purchased, and houses obtained
In the height of the season not easily gained;
So straight to their shelter the party repair
To shed all their clothing and part of their hair;
For when to the beach Beauty goes on a train,
She must part with her locks ere she trusts to
    the main.
'Tis well that poor Love is proverbially blind,
For 'twixt the rude sea and the blustering wind,
Pale Beauty, disheveled and stripped of each art,
Is surely no sight for a sensitive heart;
As witness the show from morning till noon
Of belles reft of chignon, of panier, and bloom,
Reduced to the limits by Nature provided,
Not always becoming the thin and slab-sided.

But now, from their boxes emerging, we see
Our party all ready equipped for the sea.
Good heavens! Can these be the queens of
    croquet,
Or those the spruce beaux of bewitching Broad-
    way?
The ladies are robed in flame-colored red,
Quite paling the fires of Poodle's soft head,

With a trimming of braid, three rows on the
     skirt,
And trousers to match, like a Bloomerite flirt;
But our hero's thin legs in a blue flanel case,
Resemble a monkey's got up for a race,
Or a skeleton form from a medical school,
While Gus plays the clown like a natural fool.
The footmen both snicker, the coachman looks
     grim,
But relaxes a little as Poodle goes in.
With a run, and a skip, and a faint little scream,
In a few moments more 'mid the crowd they
     are seen,
Who go bobbing like corks on the crest of the
     sea,
Or duck when the incoming breaker swings free.

What wonder we laugh as we stand on the
     shore!
Yon doctored divine might inspire our awe,
But now, in old breeches and battered sea-hat,
You can only remark his exuberant fat,
As, like an old porpoise, he awkwardly blows
(We are sketching from fancy) his bibulous
     nose.

How they danced, how they shouted, and tum-
     bled about,
Were long to relate, but at length they came
     out;
The ladies cerulean, but not in their clothes,

And Fitz P. with a chill from his head to his
  toes.
Then swift to their houses they speedily fly;
Let us hope that no curious cynic is nigh,
To scan the fair creatures with critical eye.

At length from their closets once more they
  emerge :
Can these be the figures we saw in the surge?
Has Fannie grown fat, and Carlotta found bloom,
Though ghastly before as a ghost from the tomb?
Now into the carriage and back to the hill
Ere the white flag go down, and the men take
  their fill
Of breasting the ocean in Nature's own dress;
A garb that the poor might have reason to
  bless,
Were the climate more mild, or the audience
  less,
But gone out of fashion since Eve took to
  working,
And sewed up her fig-leaves by way of a curtain.

The season has crept to the hot August days,
When the landscape lies soft 'neath the silvery
  haze,
And o'er the blue billows the gray vapors creep
On the wings of the breeze from the wastes of
  the deep.
What wonder old Newport attracts the gay
  throng!

What wonder the weary ones ardently long
To escape the gay city's sirocco and heat,
The turmoil of business, the crowd of the street,
The jar of its bustle, the strife of its ways,
Its long, sultry nights, and its thrice fervent
    days,
To find by our bright waves the *dolce-far-niente*,
And a place to deplete if your cash be too plenty.

To return to our mutton — the Frenchman is
    right,
'Tis a phrase for our hero close-fitting and tight;
A poor silly sheep to be speedily shorn,
Though few for his shearing may honestly mourn.
But a truce to this trifling; so lest we should
    tire,
We beg to present Mrs. Snobby Pariah —
A lady substantial in person and dollars,
Though perhaps not the best of grammatical
    scholars.
As a crusty old fellow was heard to remark
(There's somebody always to snap and to bark),
He'd venture the thought, though hastily thrown,
" She spoke every language excepting her own."
But an ample excuse, we know, will be voted,
When Mrs. Pariah's beginnings are quoted.
A chimney-sweep's daughter, in factory life
She worked as a maid, ere they made her a
    wife ;
And 'tis said when Pariah popped out his pro-
    posal,

Putting himself at her instant disposal,
She took twenty-four hours the case to decide
'Twixt the dressmaker's trade and the wreath of
        a bride.
It seems her decision turned out for the best,
For Pariah waxed rich, and good luck did the
        rest,
While Mrs. Pariah, in fashion's gay crowd,
Sailed a frigate, saluting in style rather loud,
With colors, and streamers, and other gay things,
Not to mention a hat with a garnish of wings.
But a dash of the factory hangs round her still,
A flavor e'en cash cannot banish at will;
As fawned on, and flattered, and flurried along,
The pleasant amusement and jest of the throng,
She shakes out her feathers, and turns up her
        nose,
Like a pig when the wind of the hurricane
        blows;
Ah! little she thinks, as she gives herself airs,
That the low "common people," at whom she
        thus stares,
Have a way of remembering things of the past,
And this sort of style makes it likely to last.


Now Mrs. Pariah — old P. was just nothing,
Save a bank and a butt for continual bluffing —
Determined to give, perhaps for that reason,
A *fête* to eclipse every ball of the season.
The cards were all out, and Fitz Poodle invited;
Of the Arams and Redower neither were
        slighted.

The thing proved successful; Pariah displayed
A grace that quite rivaled her favorite maid;
Though the coachman declared, " Our old woman
        was looking
As red round the gills as if she'd been cooking."

But 'tis not with Pariah our Muse has to do ;
We have chosen a hero, and hope to prove
        true ;
So leave to your fancy each full *matinée*,
The concerts by night and the boating by day,
The music and dust of the drive to the Fort,
With other diversions, for cash to be bought,
To all their gay doings persistently dumb,
Though the *fête* of Pariah die sad and unsung.

In a spot well defended in flank and in rear,
Where the coyest of maids could have nothing
        to fear,
And a lover might " pop," if he felt so inclined,
Nor dread some impertinent puppy behind,
There, there in that bower, with blossoms agleam,
Like Love 'mid the roses, Fitz Poodle was seen ;
Nor alone did he sit, but close pressed to his
        side
Sat Carlotta, his promised and possible bride ;
For the girl was no fool, and had tickled his
        brain,
No difficult task when 'tis shallow and vain,
And stirred the small heart that just matched
        with his head,

Till the fellow forgot that its color was red.
In short, he was led like a pup by his chain;
She was training her Poodle with might and
      with main,
To fetch and to carry, and even to beg,
Though, unlike Columbus, 'twas not her first
      egg.
She had practiced before in more difficult cases,
And laid in a stock of emotion and graces —
Could weep in a hurry, or get up a fit;
We hope that the biter may never be bit.

For a while let us wander away from the pair
To Redower and Fan, who are taking the air
Where a nice little terrace looks over the sea,
In a place made for *two*, but too little for *three*.
He stoops, and she listens with eyelids down-
      cast;
The look on her face would be pleasant to last,
A something that lights it, as if from within —
Love's own magic lantern, when not made of *tin*.
His words are quite broken, but still we may
      guess
The depth of devotion he seeks to express.
There's a language full common, and old as
      the world,
Comprehended wherever a flag is unfurled;
There's no mountain so high, no valley so deep,
Where that tongue may not move us to smile
      or to weep.
'Tis the language unspoken of lips and of eyes,

The first one e'er born, and the last one that
    dies ;
The story of Eden, that never grows old,
Yet yields nothing new, though a thousand times
    told.

'Twill be seen that our party have somewhat
    progressed
Since we saw them afloat on old Ocean's rude
    breast,
Or rather adrift, with a wave for a pillow,
And a cool bathing-tub in the trough of the
    billow ;
But boating, and driving, and walks on the
    cliff,
Not to mention their daily matutinal dip,
Had brought the affair to this fortunate close,
Notwithstanding poor Poodle's exuberant nose ;
But Carlotta had scruples, in spite of papa,
Not to speak of the lectures received from
    mamma,
Ere she yielded her charms to even a catch,
Though all deemed Fitz Poodle an excellent
    match.
Still, in spite of her fondness for horses and
    dash,
He gained his fair charmer at last by a smash —
A regular breakdown — unknown e'en to Fan,
Whose principal agent of course was a man ;
A Count, with a ribbon and arrogant air,
From Turkey, or Texas, or Tophet knows where,

With snaky black eyes and a twisted moustache,
Whose debts were apparent, more so than his
    cash,
Who fished for Carlotta, and baited his hook —
For to do the Count justice he talked like a
    book —
With romance and flattery, commingled with
    tales
Of hardships and exile, of battles and gales.

So Carlotta was won, the elopement all planned,
But the Count came in haste his ring to de-
    mand,
When at the last moment he suddenly found
His hopes of her fortune all dashed to the
    ground:
For old Aram had been a lame duck in his day,
And living on credit don't generally pay.

Meanwhile poor Carlotta had given her heart;
Though artful and tricky, the tear-drops would
    start,
When she thought of the man — a barber at
    home —
With whom she was willing the wide world to
    roam.
'Tis pity some pedagogue, versed in rattan,
Could not give a hint to that no-a-Count man,
For a fellow who chatters and swindles by rule,
Should learn of the rod in Severity's school.

Thus Poodle was blessed through his *barber*-ous
    rival,
At least when she found him beginning to
    trifle,
For a maid disappointed is willing to choose
Where before she determined to flout and
    refuse;
But alas for the swain who a *vacuum* fills,
As a possible cure for positive ills!

So the ladies were wooed, not " married and a',"
For as yet the affair was unknown to papa—
Not Aram indeed, who would ne'er have ob-
    jected,
But one with whom Fitz was more closely con-
    nected, —
For James Peter was absent, with men of the
    ring,
To get up a *corner*, and make a sure thing;

3

'Twas true a few thousands would lose, but who
    cares?
What are Poverty's groans to the bulls and the
    bears?
So he'd gone with his friends to manipulate
    gold,
And smash the poor sinners left out in the cold.
For 'twas thought if the Government cash was
    controlled,
'Twould pay for the keen ones to buy it and
    hold
Till it rose to the tune of a hundred per cent.,
When the bulls would *unload* at the top of their
    bent,
While the market was stocked at their sovereign
    pleasure,
Or kept short of funds in Custom House treas-
    ure;
But to do the thing well, there were wires to
    pull,
A Bear to be trained, and likewise a Bull, —
An uncertain menagerie e'en at the best,
The curse of our country, a national pest;
Moreover, 'twould help if the President's fame
Could be tarnished awhile by the use of his
    name,
And a certain great dealer in steamboats and
    stocks
Tie up all the gold by that safest of locks, —
The promise that Grant should not hammer the
    ring

When the traps were all baited and ready to
    spring.
But our Muse may not dwell on the pumping
    and sounding ;
Let the rogues lay their plans, and Grant do
    the pounding.
So back to our lovers we go with a fling,
And farewell awhile to the men of the ring.

Their courting went on in the old fashioned way,
With dancing by night, and coquetting by day ;
'Tis strange, while in most things the world is
    progressing,
No new patent's out in the way of caressing ;
For on Adam and Eve we may hardly improve ;
'Tis the old story still, though the centuries
    move ;
So for little endearments, and sweet honeyed
    words,
With billings and cooings, — we quote from the
    birds, —
We leave them to fancy, no mighty exertion,
When most people take to this kind of diversion.

'Mid other amusements 'twas planned they
    should go
For a trip to the Lime Rocks, and possible
    row —
Should Miss Ida prove gracious, and winds
    gently blow —
In the *Rescue*, a boat by that heroine won,

As a sort of reminder of what she had done,
For saving twelve lives — though one was a
    fleece, —
Pulling them out at a hundred apiece.
We don't mean to say that she did it for gain,
But this being written, 'tis well to explain, —
That folks came by thou ands to question and
    stare,
To fill the small parlor, and even the stair,
And beset the poor girl by night and by day;
Till, weary and sick, she was going away,
And then gave a pitiful thousand in all,
To pay her for working through summer and
    fall;
For the life-saving business proved easier far,
Than playing the public's particular star.

The day was well chosen, the breezes in tune,
And the ladies looked sweet as the roses of
    June;
So lest their arrangements with others might
    clash,
Fitz Poodle had hired a boat of old Ash,
A captain renowned in the little craft way,
For sailing " Ye Maidens " o'er billow and bay.
Then quick to the landing, in haste to embark,
Our party all drove, in the mood for a lark;
For though timid on water, the girls seldom
    fail
With laughter and shout to get into a gale.
There were bundles and baskets of grub to be
    shipped,

There were shrieks if the sail-boat was suddenly
      tipped,
With just the least blushing when called to dis-
      close
Of a neat-fitting gaiter much more than the
      toes ;
For their ankles were good, though their figures
      were bad, —
A promise unfilled that's decidedly sad ;
For 'tis Nature's own outward and visible sign,
The show-window card, if the form be divine ;
For even the hand may be judged by the foot ;
If the gauntlet be little, why so is the boot.
But enough of æsthetics ; while the gay party
      start,
We'll bring to a period our lecture on art.

At length they are off, with a cheer and a shout,
And a waving of kerchiefs that fluttered about ;
With the wind right abaft to the Lime Rocks
      they ran,
But still kept their course as suggested by Fan,
Intending to coast by Conanicut's shore,
And, unless the young ladies should deem it a
      bore,
To visit old Beaver Tail Light, and then stop
On their way back to town at Miss Ida's small
      dock.
How the visit was made, how Fitz acted silly,
How Fannie turned sick, and Carlotta felt chilly,
How Redower's legs got entwined in a rope

That almost extinguished the German's best
    hope,
We doubt not were written by Ash in his log;
But this much we know, they were caught in
    a fog,
With a thin driving mist and a spatter of rain,
A fact by the Arams remembered with pain;
For bonnets cost money, and when short of
    cash,
To boat in your best is decidedly rash.


Now on their return 'twas discussed and ap-
    proved,
And a vote of the house was accordingly moved,
That on the next night, at the Ocean House
    hop,
All parties should meet at the party to stop,
Till each took a turn, and perhaps a turnover,
In which case an action would soon lie for
    trover,
In that maze so divine of twisting and squirm-
    ing, —
A giddy go round if the pupil be learning.
But the heads of our lovers, though silly and
    weak,
Would have scorned to complain, though they
    danced for a week;
Though stupid enough where the brain had a
    hand in,
"At least in their legs they'd a strong under-
    standing."

At ten of the clock, on the evening appointed,
Our beaux, by their barbers all newly anointed,
Drove up to the Ocean House steps with a
    whirl,
Each fully content with his favorite girl.
The Arams caused quite a sensation that night,
Though the ladies declared them a horrible
    fright ;
For Carlotta was robed in ruby red silk,
And Fannie in satin the color of milk ;
Their get-up was stunning; e'en Mrs. Pariah,
Whose head wore a helmet suggestive of fire,
Confessed herself vanquished when Fannie ap-
    peared
With Augustus Redower, all neck-tie and beard.

'Twas a scene for a painter, at least a reporter,
Or one not too chary of sister or daughter,
To view the girls languish, and see the men
    squeeze,
While brothers and fathers looked on at their
    ease ;
But alas for the husband by jealousy damned,
Watching his wife by each roué eye scanned,
While her points and her paces are fully dis-
    cussed,
And not even her character suffered to rust.
God help the world ! if mothers and wives
Are to waste in such follies the morn of their
    lives,
While duties neglected cry loudly at home,

And the babe in its cradle makes sorrowful
　　moan.
Yet steadily sweeping the fashion tide still
Flows through the long hall with its tremu-
　　lous thrill,
Till the night air grows heavy and faint with
　　perfume,
And the dancers seem flowers of tropical bloom,
With diamonds like dew-drops to hang on each
　　belle, —
Not all of them paid for, as jewelers tell.
And the waltz! O, that wonderful waltz! where
　　the heels
Of thrice active Redower made magical reels,
Till a boarder declared — the impudent lubber —
His legs were a compound of breeches and
　　rubber;
While Carlotta, with dark flowing hair, went the
　　pace,
With soft sliding step, and each languishing
　　grace,
Though her eyes caught full many an amorous
　　glance,
As sustained by Fitz Poodle, she swept through
　　the dance;
And Fannie, who feels she is looking her best
In the arms of Redower seems perfectly blest.

Of Bullion the banker, with velvet and squint,
The satirical pen might flow without stint, —
Whose horses and flunkies, bright buttons and
　　bays,

Quite rival the circus in various ways;
For the clown seldom rides with his roystering
    crew,
While in Bullion's big wagon he's always on
    view.
'Tis quite a sensation to see them dash by,
Though some view the turn-out with critical eye.
At the footmen, at least, no cynic should frown,
As, with buttons beplastered, and coat-tails hung
    down,
Their livery aids to prevent the mistake,
More frequent than pleasant, of those who might
    take
The man for the master, and thus spoil the plan
Of the party who ride in this small caravan.
'Tis said that the dash is all on the street,
That the servants complain there is little to eat,
That the cook finds her reckoning kept to a dot,
And woe to the clerk who a ledger should blot.
But enough of our Bullion; we cherish the
    name,
And expect to subscribe to his posthumous fame,
By placing a *statue*, perhaps in the Park,
At which no impertinent puppy may bark,
(Near the one by our princely Belmont just
    erected,
In which, like its donor, no flaw is detected,)
Whose brass so enduring, or gray island stone,
For slights of the past should amply atone;
And while we'd not dictate, or seem to com-
    mand,

We'd suggest to the artist, a wide open hand;
But whether extended to give or receive,
To those who best know him we willingly leave.
An inscription might follow, both plain and
    terse,
If fifty per cent. could be woven in verse.
Yet the lines we annex might be made to suf-
    fice,
Though unworthy the theme they are truthfully
    nice :

## IN MEMORIAM.

Here *lies* — how appropriate — Bullion the banker,
For whom all who miss him persistently hanker;
So devoted a husband, so tender, so true,
In an infidel age was refreshing to view ;
As a master unrivaled, forbearing, and kind,
To his debts ever prompt, to his dues almost
    blind ;
This marble, put up by his friends of the street,
Bears witness his spirit was gracious and sweet;
Enough — be it written in letters *de oro*,
"Hic jacet vir nulla non donandus lauro."

Thus much of description — and less might have
    done,
But 'tis hard to leave off when once you've
    begun —
Is meant as a preface, though not very brief,
To a new episode of our subject in chief.

Mrs. B. gave a party quite striking and new,
To flutter each fop on the long avenue ;
For *tableaux vivants* were the principal treat,
Where the faces make up for the absence of
    feet.
We don't mean the feet that bipeds must walk in,
But the feat that's involved in ranting and
    talking ;
A very bad jest, and as badly expressed ;
We refer you to Miller (not Hugh) for the rest.
To this party exclusive our friends were invited,
With the Count, and some Englishman recently
    knighted,
With other bright stars of the upper-ten world,
That realm *recherche*, all beflounced and be-
    curled.
So our lovers decided, blow high or blow low,
To the Bullions' grand party they'd certainly go.
Moreover, Carlotta and Fitz were to take
A part in the *tableau* intended to make
The sensation *par excellence*, high and supreme ;
Let us hope the *dénouement* may realize their
    dream.
The picture referred to involved a live goose,
Whose uproar saved Rome from fagot and noose ;
For such were the horrors, and worse, of a sack,
When the enemy crept to their midnight attack.
For the fowl caught a glimpse of some form
    that looked ill,
Then cackled so loudly, the guard on the hill,
Aroused by the clamor, sprang quick to his feet,

And forced the armed foe to a speedy retreat;
Though the story be new to boys fresh from
        college,
'Tis a trite one to graybeards in classical
        knowledge.
For further particulars, apply to Liddel,
Who to honor the goose which once cackled so
        well,
Spins a yarn rather tough, and quite hard to
        believe,
Of some soldiers so pious they saw fit to leave
To a goddess, one Juno, by way of a treat,
A fine flock of fowls, though they'd nothing to
        eat.
Yet we fancy no priest of her temple grew thin,
Though to dine off of goose were a *capital* sin.
So the scene was selected, but only the goose
Was permitted his voluble tongue to let loose,
While the rest of the figures stood speechless
        and dumb,
For the better inspection of all who might come;
With a background of sentries alarmed or
        asleep,
Where a maiden and matron should *silently* weep,
Parts left to Carlotta, and Mrs. Aram;
While Fitz Poodle played goose as instructed by
        Fan.
How he practiced and cackled until he was
        hoarse,
And studied from nature, are matters of course,
With an old speckled bird exciting his dander,

Till he fairly wore out the unfortunate gander,
Not to mention a mask like a huge feather bed,
With a yellowish bill, and a long goosey head.

The evening came round, and the audience too;
Carlotta wears tunic of wonderful hue,
In longitude scant, like the " Ledger's " last text,
" The rest of this *tail* will be found in our next."
While the Count as her backer, with buckler
     and bill,
Stood for Manlius roused from his sleep on the
     hill.
But the goose after all was the star of the night,
Till, sad to relate, to our hero's great fright,
His false head fell off, and his real one appeared,
With the faint English whiskers by way of a
     beard;
While between, like a lantern that hangs in a
     bush,
You could see his eyes peep, and his ruby nose
     blush.
The curtain fell quick, mid a burst of applause;
But alas for Fitz Poodle, the innocent cause,
Who, while cursing his stars, and unfortunate
     luck,
Was christened anew, the Red-headed Duck.
So ended the farce, and Carlotta retired,
An event by our hero extremely desired;
For to wait as a *butt* when you came *butt* to
     shoot,
Is insult and injury added to boot.

Our story has lingered too long by the way;
We haste to conclude without further delay:
An elopement was planned the world to deceive,
Not that Aram papa would exceedingly grieve;
But as Poodle James P. was just then Major
    Ursa,
The job was confided in quiet to Curser;
No flourish of trumpets or flourish of tongues,
No bills for *trousseau* to bring about duns;
But a quiet affair, with a witness to prove
They stood for each other, — their promise to
    love.
So the bargain was made, and the articles sold,
Depending, alas, on a corner in gold,
Though of this the young ladies are yet to be
    told;
But both of them promise to take and to keep,
While Fannie alone looks ready to weep;
For Carlotta seems iced, with a curl on her
    lip —
She had talked with the Count ere she ventured
    the trip.
But now before Heaven, "in sickness and
    health,"
'Neath poverty's frown, or the fullness of wealth,
" Till death them do part," she vows she will
    cling,
To what she well knows is a poor brainless
    thing.
Will her heart keep the vow that her lips doth
    record ?

Will the spirit find rest that so lately hath
    warred ?
Ask not of the future its secrets to tell —
But hark to the sound of the steamer's last
    bell.

They are off, but their fancies take different
    ways:
While the Poodles go North, on Niagara to gaze,
Augustus considers the air of "The Hub,"
Not to mention his father — ah, there comes the
    rub, —
Might require his presence at least to disclose
The match as yet secret, and under the rose.
And now ere we drop them for aye from our
    story,
We'll sum them up briefly like "old Mother
    Morey."
His father declined the pair to support,
And even Redower's allowance cut short;
So he proves that extremes may frequently meet,
By *working* his jaws through the *play* of his feet;
In a word, he's turning his legs to account,
And now receives pupils to any amount,
With Mrs. Redower, who helps fill the purse;
But lately her spirits have changed for the
    worse,
Though expecting a pupil, a lively one too,
For whose better reception she now has in view
A neat little wardrobe, quite small at the best,
With worked under-clothes and diminutive vest;

At which, while the fiddle is going without,
She patiently toils with some little doubt,
If business should fail, or matters grow worse.
What figure Augustus might cut as a nurse.

Meanwhile the Fitz Poodles are off on a *train*,
A double one too, though the meaning is plain,
They have rolled through the Sound on the
  Admiral's boat,
With music to keep you awake while afloat,
Where Fisk reigns omnipotent, great in his
  wealth;
He has dealt in his gold till he's gilded himself,
While his virtues reflected shine out in the
  brass,
Which begins with the Captain, and ends with
  the gas.
So the pair rattle on with a jerk and a jar,
Quite natural too, for we seldom go far
On a journey by rail, or a trip with a wife,
Without that slight swerving so common in life,
Which is seen on the stage in " Family Jars,"
And is equally felt in " A Ride on the Cars."
But Niagara is reached with its thundering roar;
A carriage obtained; they stand at the door
Of a first-class hotel, where Poodle goes in,
In clothes superfine and a large diamond pin,
Despite of Carlotta, who fain would repress,
With a taste better bred, his monkeyfied dress.
So behold them all settled, yet strange to relate,
The Count reached the town by a train rather
  late,

And more singular far, "had happened to
    glance
At their registered names — a fortunate chance,"
Which enabled that snaky-eyed exile to take
A room for the present, — "indeed he might
    make
His stay quite as long as the Poodles should
    stop;"
Then glanced at Carlotta, who blushed and
    spoke not.
So the time sped along. Fitz Poodle soon found
His enjoyment consisted in circling round,
Mid billiards and bars, with horses and grooms,
While the Count and Carlotta would chat in his
    rooms.
At length when his purse is depleted and low,
He is driven by need to James Peter to go;
So sits down to pencil a note to "*mon pere*,"
Who thus far had honored the drafts of his
    heir.
He wrote, "I dare say you're astonished to
    see,
And wonder why I at Niagara should be;
But in fact, my Paternal, I've just settled down,
And cut all the vices, so low, of the town, —
You know the old rule if a rake should reform,
He makes the best husband that ever was
    born;
If this should prove true, my Carlotta is blessed,
But send me a thousand, and don't mind the
    rest.

I'll drop in ere long, in a sociable way
(By by, old Gov.) when convenient to stay,
But just now Carlotta don't care for the sea ;
With love from my spouse, your devoted Fitz P."
To this came an answer like telegram terse,
" I can't send the money, Fitz Poodle, I'm burst ;
I leave by the steamer; my margin's rubbed out ;
You must shift for yourself; I can't e'en give
    my route."

Fitz Poodle was ruined; bad news travels fast ;
'Tis vain to repent of extravagance past ;
But was it not worse that his wife should elope
With the Count, and her jewels, his ultimate
    hope ?
Fitz Poodle was missed; 'twas supposed that he
    fell,
But of this no observer the story could tell ;
Yet certain it is that his body was found
Where the waltz of the whirlpool goes merrily
    round.
It may be the man, though erring and wild,
Deep down in his heart kept one well undefiled,
The love he had staked on his false wife, and
    lost,
To leave him a wreck on the wave tempest
    tossed,
Till despairing of life, and forgetful of God,
He sought a cold pillow beneath the green sod,
With coward heart hoping in rest of the grave
To escape a disaster he dared not to brave.

And Carlotta the perjured — how fares it with
    her?
Has Memory no power that false soul to stir;
Has Conscience no hold on the heart that so
    lied
To the husband who honestly made her his
    bride?
Though polluted e'en then by the serpent's foul
    breath,
She vowed to prove faithful, and true to the
    death.
Though so near with her lover, she heard not
    the doom
Of the mate left to perish in blackness of
    gloom,
While she found with the Count a poor dwell-
    ing beside
The river that sweeps with Niagara's full tide.
She was walking far down by the brink of the
    stream,
In idle mood watching its bright eddies gleam,
When the wave flung a corpse on the shore at
    her feet,
Tossing the dead arm as if it would greet
With a gesture of welcome the foul faithless
    wife,
Who a brief space before had caressed it in
    life.
The shock was too great, and reason dethroned,
For the sin of the past, if it might be atoned.
Yet ever in madness she walks by the stream,

And  sees  the  pale  corpse  with  its  hollow  eyes
        gleam,
While  the  white  ghostly  fingers  seem  beckoning
        still,
Clutching  her  own  with  their  terrible  thrill;
For  the  spoiler  who  now  should  have  guarded
        her  best,
Leaves  his  victim  'mid  strangers  to  rave  or  to
        rest,
And  goes  with  the  jewels  which  most  he  could
        prize, —
For  purity  ne'er  was  a  gem  in  his  eyes;
The  flower  once  gathered,  was  soon  thrown  aside,
For  he  valued  the  widow  e'en  less  than  the  bride;
But  fled  with  his  gains — the  tale  is  of  old, —
A  slave  to  his  lust,  and  still  more  to  his  gold.

Though  Justice  moves  slowly,  she's  sure  in  the
        end;
As  witness  an  "invite"  the  Count  has  to  spend
A  few  years  to  come  at  a  quiet  retreat,
Where  every  arrangement,  though  simple,  is
        neat,
And  ill-disposed  people  kept  *out*  by  a  grating,
Are  constantly  watched  by  servants  in  waiting;
For  the  host  is  so  jealous  he  never  can  bear
That  his  guests  should  feel  lonely  while  taking
        the  air.
So  a  careful  companion  is  always  provided,
To  whose  constant  attention  the  inmate's  con-
        fided,

As clothed in a uniform, coarse but complete,
He shuffles along with his iron-clad feet.
An order of merit he fain would decline,
Were talking permitted by word or by sign.
Moreover, the Count has been trying the *bathing*,
Though greatly opposed to the cutting and
    shaving.

## GRACE AFTER MEAT.

THE vision has fled; like a dream of the night
The actors and actresses passed out of sight;
The drop curtain falls, and my fancy forms melt,
Like the nebulous stars of the lacteal belt,
When the day dawn creeps coldly above the
   dark hill,
And the breath of the morning the night vapors
   thrill.
Nor fancy the figures my wand has thus raised,
To be characters living, on which you have
   gazed.
They are met with each day in city or mart,
The silly in head, and corrupted in heart.
Nor suppose that the poor and the mean are
   exempt,
That 'tis only to Lazarus talents are lent
Of justice and purity, honor and truth,
Abiding in age, as implanted in youth.
All these may be found mid the wealthy and
   learned;
God heeds not the altar where incense is burned;
Though the censer be jeweled, or hewn from
   the stone,
The All-seeing regards the oblation alone.

There are hands ever open by riches made full,
While the poorer man's purse his heart-strings
  may pull;
There is meanness in low life as well as in high,
The proud, scornful lip, and the arrogant eye.
We are all of us failing; e'en Charity needs
The prayer "Help me, Lord," as the saint tells
  her beads.
Then this be our motto, mid folly and pride,
Remember the mansion we're walking beside,
Whose roof is of sod, and its fashion of old,
With earth for a pillow, and dust to enfold,
Where the night is unbroken, the season the
  same,
And the sleeper unmindful of honor or shame.
Then pause for a moment, in Fashion's gay tide,
In the mansions you build by the blue water
  side;
There's rebuke in each billow that breaks 'neath
  the cliff,
There's a tremulous story on Ocean's white lip,
As it falls into foam, and the wild waters moan,
For it speaks of an Ocean more vast than its
  own, —
A sea that is shoreless, yet silent and still,
To which we go down, let us strive as we will;
Where the rich and the poor, the high and the
  low,
Are lost mid its solemn mysterious flow;
Where humanity meets unstripped of its pride,
Save its record with God, and nothing beside.